THE APPLE TART OF EDEN

A DEITIES ANONYMOUS STORY

M. L. BUCHMAN

Buchman Bookworks

M.L. Buchman is guaranteed to get me lost in a good story.

— THE READING CAFE, WAY OF THE
WARRIOR: NSDQ

I love Buchman's writing. His vivid descriptions bring everything to life in an unforgettable way.

— PURE JONEL, HOT POINT

Other works by M. L. Buchman:

White House Protection Force

Off the Leash
On Your Mark
In the Weeds

The Night Stalkers
MAIN FLIGHT
The Night Is Mine
I Own the Dawn
Wait Until Dark
Take Over at Midnight
Light Up the Night
Bring On the Dusk
By Break of Day
WHITE HOUSE HOLIDAY
Daniel's Christmas
Frank's Independence Day
Peter's Christmas
Zachary's Christmas
Roy's Independence Day
Damien's Christmas
AND THE NAVY
Christmas at Steel Beach
Christmas at Peleliu Cove
5E
Target of the Heart
Target Lock on Love
Target of Mine
Target of One's Own

Firehawks
MAIN FLIGHT
Pure Heat
Full Blaze
Hot Point
Flash of Fire
Wild Fire
SMOKEJUMPERS
Wildfire at Dawn
Wildfire at Larch Creek
Wildfire on the Skagit

Delta Force
Target Engaged
Heart Strike
Wild Justice
Midnight Trust

Where Dreams
Where Dreams are Born
Where Dreams Reside
Where Dreams Are of Christmas
Where Dreams Unfold
Where Dreams Are Written

Eagle Cove
Return to Eagle Cove
Recipe for Eagle Cove
Longing for Eagle Cove
Keepsake for Eagle Cove

Henderson's Ranch
Nathan's Big Sky
Big Sky, Loyal Heart
Big Sky Dog Whisperer

Love Abroad
Heart of the Cotswolds: England
Path of Love: Cinque Terre, Italy

Dead Chef Thrillers
Swap Out!
One Chef!
Two Chef!

Deities Anonymous
Cookbook from Hell: Reheated
Saviors 101

SF/F Titles
The Nara Reaction
Monk's Maze
the Me and Elsie Chronicles

Strategies for Success (NF)
Managing Your Inner Artist/Writer
Estate Planning for Authors

Short Story Series by M. L. Buchman:

<u>The Night Stalkers</u>
The Night Stalkers
The Night Stalkers 5E
The Night Stalkers CSAR
The Night Stalkers Wedding Stories

<u>Firehawks</u>
The Firehawks Lookouts
The Firehawks Hotshots
The Firebirds

<u>Delta Force</u>
Delta Force Short Stories

<u>US Coast Guard</u>
US Coast Guard

<u>White House Protection Force</u>
White House Protection Force Short Stories

<u>Where Dreams</u>
Where Dreams Short Stories

<u>Eagle Cove</u>
Eagle Cove Short Story

<u>Henderson's Ranch</u>
Henderson's Ranch Short Stories

<u>Dead Chef Thrillers</u>
Dead Chef Short Stories

<u>Deities Anonymous</u>
Deities Anonymouse Short Stories

<u>SF/F Titles</u>
The Future Night Stalkers
Single Titles

The pounding in the back of the deli echoed the pounding in Anne's head. Retired gods and goddesses weren't supposed to get colds, but this one had certainly slammed their household. She and Joshua had finally closed up the deli and retreated to their upstairs apartment, because there were limits after all—even if she was the one who always had to set them.

But tomorrow was Rosh Hashanah and a Jewish deli couldn't be closed for the Jewish New Year.

She rubbed at her aching forehead, surprised as always not to find her crown there. She hadn't worn the thing in over two millennia, and still she missed it. There were times she wished she'd kept it, but it had been much more satisfying to heave it in Zeus' face when she'd dumped his sorry behind. After all, it wasn't being married to him that had made her the Mother Goddess Hera; that had been by divine right from Mom and Dad. Well, Mom anyway. Dad had been something of a jerk as well. *Why do we always marry in our father's image?* Pointless path that she wasn't going to think about again…until next time.

After booting Zeus and his latest gaggle of sycophantic nymphs off Mount Olympus, Hera had played around a bit, but ultimately moved in with the One God.

She only regretted doing so whenever he was sick—Joshua could be such *qvetch* when he was ill. *Oy vey,* did that man know how to complain. But he was a sweetie at heart.

Anne moved the hands of the plastic clock-sign on the front door to announce they were opening again at noon. Six hours would be plenty of time to set everything to rights. Normally she could do it faster, but it was her first day back on her feet and she wasn't feeling any too quick about it.

She'd started going by "Anne"—the French form of Hannah, which was close enough, but not too close to Hera—shortly after they'd opened a nice Jewish deli out in the countryside not far from Paris. They rode out the Crusades right through the Dark Ages and the Age of Exploration there. Louis had built Versailles nearby and he often stopped in for a cuppa and a piece of rugelach. She'd loved France, but the bloody revolution had been too reminiscent of the testosterone-poisoned Spartans for her taste.

Seattle was a nice change. A little rustic at first, but it had very few wars and even fewer guillotines.

Joshua was still down with the cold—indulging his sniffles as if he was a mortal and his life was ending—but Anne had come down to the deli to tend to the things that couldn't wait. Without much hope she told her lingering headache to please go away because she couldn't face taking another pill or one more swallow some sickly sweet syrup—Nyquil was so completely not the nectar of the Gods.

The cool morning glittered beyond the rain-washed windows. The trees of Ravenna Boulevard had soaked up all of the Seattle sunshine they were going to receive for a while, and were now contemplating the long rains of fall. That reminded her, Persephone soon would be returning to her winter home as Queen of the Underworld beside that old letch Pluto. Anne really must remember to go visit her before she went back to Hades for the winter—snowbirding was fine, but Pluto kept the thermostat far too high for Anne's taste.

The pounding against the back room delivery door started again; she'd forgotten about it. There was a desperate need for coffee, so she quickly started a pot as she crossed behind the long glassed-in case that would soon be brimming with potato salad, knishes, carrot cake, and other Jewish delicacies.

"I'm coming. I'm coming," she shouted out and then wished she hadn't when her headache swelled to proportions she'd thought only Zeus could ever produce. Maybe she *should* go back to bed.

Past the pickle barrel, which her nose was still too stuffed up to smell, and through the swinging doors into the back storeroom which swooshed back and forth behind her.

She unbolted the rear delivery door…but there was no one there. No one driving away up or down the narrow alley. The backyards of houses, parked cars, the deli's

Dumpster and recycle bins. The alley was empty except for Myrtle Thomas who waved a greeting as she raced the engine on her Toyota Corolla. She might look like everyone's favorite granny, but she drove with all the panache of Apollo racing his chariot across the heavens and far more style.

Inside the deli, the banging continued.

Anne traced it to behind a pile of boxes a few steps along the kitchen's rear wall. She unstacked several cases of sauerkraut, another of #10 cans of beets, and several cases of those little plastic knives for when customers wanted their bagel and cream cheese to go.

Behind all of those she unearthed a small door, half the size of a normal one. It looked to be carved of a single great slab of wood. She ran a quick hand over the rough surface. Applewood? This hadn't been here before. At least not that she could recall.

The beating on the other side continued.

Rather than a knob or a lock, there was simply a handle carved right into the wood.

She pulled on it.

The miniature door swung open and sunlight flooded into the deli's kitchen and storeroom. Sunlight wrapped in the smells of the harvest. Apple and pear, hazelnut and pomegranate swept into the kitchen and danced merrily in the corners. The sun from this door had an entirely different quality than the wet glitter of the Seattle sunshine. It washed away her headache and the last of her chills.

What in Hade—

"About time," a gruff voice snarled from beyond the

threshold. A small man sat cross-legged on the dirt, rubbing at his knuckles as if to see whether or not they had been damaged by his prolonged beating on the door. He was perhaps the leanest man she'd ever seen: narrow-faced, arms and legs so thin they were almost vestigial. He was dirty and wore only a ragged loin cloth made of…goodness, scales. It looked quite uncomfortable.

His eyes traveled up and down her body, dwelling overlong at her chest. "Nice," he mumbled to himself. "Old Joshua finally caught himself a cute one."

"Cute? I'm not cute." As the Goddess Hera she'd been known for being one of the three great beauties of Grecian lore. She'd have been known as the *one* great beauty if Aphrodite hadn't blatantly bribed the contest judge Paris with the promise of bedding Helen of Troy. The fact that he'd turned down Hera's gift to be king of all Europe and Asia only proved how ill-chosen he was as a judge. To add insult to injury, it had been her husband Zeus who had chosen the young prat as judge in the first place.

Of course she couldn't say any of that to this wizened stranger.

"Cute," the old man insisted. "Bet you're even cuter out of those clothes. Care to prove me wrong?"

"Care to get kicked?"

"Not really," he grimaced. "I get that quite enough as it is."

"I'm so surprised."

He leered once more, but it didn't carry to his voice, "You showed your breasts enough to marble carvers and painters over the years. Why not me?" Instead he sounded sullen.

"Most of them were just making it up. The only ones who—" Anne breathed in sharply. Her vanity as a young goddess had led her to pose early on for hundreds of statues and paintings of the Goddess Hera. But Anne, wife of Joshua, was a far more discreet woman. There wasn't a single authentic depiction of her more mature years. "Wait! You know who I really am?"

"Aw, get a clue, sweet cheeks. Joshua and I go way back. Where is the lucky wretch who gets to squeeze these apples?" He made grab-and-squeeze motions toward her chest.

Anne was on the verge of slamming the door in his face, but then she caught another whiff of the harvest-scented air through the low frame. Birds sang and cooed there. Even though it shared a wall with the normal-sized delivery entrance, it opened onto a much more vibrant world. One she didn't recognize.

Beyond the narrow path of dust on which the little old man sat, lush growth flourished beneath a bright sun. It wasn't hot on her sandaled toes, but just ever so pleasantly warm. Her feet hadn't been properly warm since she'd departed Greece and left it to those callous Roman louts. Anne knew that she and hers hadn't exactly been models of decorum, but the Roman gods were truly cads.

"He's sick," though she'd roust Joshua soon despite his whining. They had a deli to run and now this little man to deal with.

"Well, if he wants his delivery, he'd better show up soon. They're ripe now."

"What are? I can take the delivery."

"No, lady, you can't."

Then he reached out a thin hand, shot a final leer at her, and pulled the applewood door shut. It slammed into place with a surprising amount of force. She tried to pull it open, she hadn't bent down to see farther through the low door and now regretted the missed opportunity.

It wouldn't budge.

CHAPTER 2

"*I*'m dying here."

"You can't die. You're immortal, remember?" Hera pulled the sheets off her husband.

He made a grab for her that proved he was far from death's door but she wasn't having any patience with that at the moment.

"Come," she captured the hand that had been aimed at her behind and used it to leverage him to his feet. "Shower and shave. There's a delivery waiting for you."

"What delivery?" he moped his way into the bathroom after she dodged his next move. She began stripping the bed to emphasize her point. Besides, after days laying abed with their two brutal colds, it was definitely time for clean sheets.

"He wouldn't say," she stuffed the sheets into the hamper. "A skinny and dirty old man."

Joshua stuck his round face back out around the door jamb, his balding pate and ruffle of white hair looked friendly and grandfatherly on him. "How dirty?"

"He made a whole thing about wanting to see my breasts."

Joshua grinned, "Can't blame him, you have great ones; especially for a woman in her fifth millennium. Want to join me in the shower?"

"Had one already this morning, dear. He was also filthy. Scrawny little man wallowing in the dust. And you have some explaining to do about…" She trailed off. Joshua's face had gone as white as his hair.

"You saw…*him?*"

"Behind the little applewood door."

"But how? No one but me can see him and…well, one other who hasn't spoken to either of us since."

"Goddess. Wife. Hello. I could see every time Zeus cheated on me just as clearly as I can see you have some explaining to do. You weren't the only god to think up the All-Seeing Eye."

"I'll be right out." And he was gone. By the sound of his morning ablutions, he was now in a hurry.

She strolled into the bathroom—tiled-marble white and lit-sunshine yellow—and called over the noise of the shower.

"Who is he?"

"What?"

Anne knew she'd spoken plenty loud enough to be heard.

She flushed the toilet.

He yelped.

Mortal plumbing did have its side benefits.

"He's nobody."

However, there was one problem with mortal

plumbing in this situation, you had to wait for the tank to refill.

She could be patient—when it suited her. So she waited.

Then she flushed again.

"Okay, okay!" he cried out in desperation. "Hold on a moment."

Much of his skin was beet red when he came out of the shower and began toweling off. He wasn't the prettiest god with his rounded shape and little Jewish belly, but he was hers and if she hadn't already stripped the sheets, she just might let him take her back to bed.

Having lost the leverage of the flushing toilet, she folded her arms, just below her breasts to emphasize them, and waited him out. He pulled on the blue underwear with white snowflakes that she'd bought him last year, then his typical gray khakis, button-down white shirt, and loafers.

She offered him a morning hug in apology and kissed him on both the cheeks.

Joshua tried to hurry off, but Anne had anticipated that move and leaned against the closed bathroom door.

"Now talk."

"I hate to keep him waiting. He's not very patient."

"A trait he shares with *your WIFE!*" She raised her voice enough that the walls bowed steeply outward. The trees along Ravenna began shedding their leaves a month early for the hard winter to come, and the Earth hiccupped in its orbit. Scientists would have a new couple hundredths of a leap-second to explain with yet more papers published about the previously undiscovered truths of quantum flux.

Joshua fetched a couple of Q-tips to clean his ears.

"Wow!" he complimented her and leaned in to give a kiss.

She accepted the kiss and caught his hand as it traveled from her backside, where it belonged, to the doorknob, where it definitely didn't. A quick twist on his pinkie made her point.

He retreated, nursing his hand.

"It's a long story."

Anne knew about his long stories. She was glad she'd started the coffee; this was definitely going to require a fresh pot.

CHAPTER 3

*J*oshua was slipperier than she'd anticipated. While Anne was preparing his coffee in his favorite ceramic mug—a misshapen old thing with the phrase *Simha,* Joy, painted on it that he'd picked up at Jericho—and toasting his bagel, he'd slipped into the back storeroom without her.

She rushed through the swinging doors and caught Joshua and the skinny old man in mid-exchange. They were on their respective sides of the applewood door, both scowling down at a basket overflowing with the most lovely apples that rested exactly half in one world and half in another.

Hera had never been a big fan of apples. Not since her daughter Eris, the Goddess of Discord, had tossed that apple "for the fairest of all" that led to the Judgment of Paris mess in the first place and the whole Trojan War disaster afterward. You didn't need to be the prophetess Cassandra to see that coming. In retrospect she felt rather bad about it.

"Good crop this year," Joshua said in a neutral voice he was rarely able to achieve.

"It was," the little man replied in a clipped tone.

"Thanks."

The man shrugged.

Men. If Hera lived to be a million, which she was going to, she'd never understand men.

"About time you introduced me," Anne moved forward causing both men to jump guiltily. She knew the One God had any number of things to be guilty about, but why was a basket of apples among them?

"Hi, Anne," Joshua looked about for an escape, but apparently couldn't find one. Besides, she was quicker on her feet than he was and he knew it.

The little man kicked at the dust.

Joshua fidgeted uncomfortably.

"Hi, Ahv!" A tiny angel popped into being and fluttered around the basket. "Is it that time of year again already?" Henrietta.

Anne did her best not to sigh too deeply. The tiny sprite always *meant* well.

Her equally tiny halo was mostly lost in her brown curly locks as she flew about and inspected the apples carefully. Finally, after a long running self-dialogue on their fine form and which Pantone color swatch they matched, she settled with a flitter of her wings to sit on the topmost one.

The ninth-order angel continued to chatter, her one great skill. "These are wonderful, Ahv. Do you remember the crop the year Cleopatra needed all that help? Awful year for apples. I can tell that these are nice and firm," she tapped a tiny bare foot on the next apple below her perch to make her point. "How did you deal with the drainage problems?"

"Drainage problems?" Joshua managed in a strained voice.

Anne had learned long since that keeping her mouth shut around the chatty little angel was the only real hope of finding a way back *out* of the conversation.

"Of course drainage problems. His orchard has taken a horrible amount of work to maintain."

"His orchard has only two trees in it."

"And the garden. Besides they're really important trees. How would you like to be fighting an infestation of beavers? Well, it's not actual beavers, but the Iraqis have dammed and undammed the Tigris and the Euphrates in so many places that…"

Anne sat down on a stack of boxes of non-dairy creamer. From here she could see to either side of the small man too thin to fill the doorframe. Beyond him she could see lush gardens rampant with growth. Blackberry vines interlaced with bush beans which were overrunning a carrot patch. And though nicely weeded, the carrot tops were wilted from overwatering.

Hand-hacked drainage ditches criss-crossed throughout the expansive garden. Two enormous old apple trees framed the background. It was hard to imagine the thin man doing all that on his own.

Henrietta had moved on to fishes and butterflies falling in love and something about only parrots being able to solve the issue.

Anne began feeling sorry for the man in the garden

and not merely because of Henrietta's suddenly lecturing on the "fruitfulness" of vegetables.

"Why don't you get some help?" Anne did her best to regain control of the conversation.

"Ask him!" Ahv jabbed a finger at her husband.

Joshua again shifted nervously from one foot to the other. He only did that when he'd done something bad.

"Joshua?"

"I might, well, have put a guard at the gate," he said the last in a great rush.

"Cherubim and a flaming sword!" Ahv hissed out.

"Oh *skatá!*" Anne didn't curse often, but at the moment she was very glad she was sitting down, even if it was on non-dairy creamer.

CHAPTER 4

"*A*hv means 'snake' in Hebrew," Anne's voice was barely a whisper as it slipped out. Her perch on the creamer was not very stable at the moment.

"Yes, it does," Henrietta agreed cheerfully. "Though in Ancient Hebrew the emphasis on the three sounds is actually—"

"That door. Those apples," too shocked to care about the risk of interrupting the angle in mid-flow, Anne talked right over her. "That's the Garden of Eden," she managed to point through the door.

"Well, of course it is, silly," Henrietta had stood up on her apple, placed tiny fists on tiny hips, and glared at Anne. "What do you think we've been talking about all this time?"

"You're the snake," she shifted where she was pointing.

"Genesis Chapter Three at your service," Ahv made a deep bow that actually rippled up the length of his body. "Though I prefer serpent if you don't mind. Show me your breasts and I'll be glad to tell you how they compared to Eve's," he tried to leer but didn't quite pull it off. He looked too sad.

"I thought the universe was created fourteen billion years ago. That's what you always told me," now she aimed her attention at Joshua. "Have you been lying to me all these years?" She didn't have good control of her voice. As she rose to her feet and began stalking toward Joshua the lids blew off several jars of honey and added to the sweet air that flowed through the low door.

"No, my dear. Not at all." Joshua stopped and looked uncertain how to continue.

"The universe," Henrietta chirped in, "*is* fourteen billion years old. There are just other myths…"

"Like your lovely self, my dear," Joshua tried to slip between Henrietta's words.

"…who were such commonly held belief systems that they become a new reality that is then integrated into the Universe."

"How can reality change like that?"

Henrietta shrugged, "Why do you think they use the Software that Runs the Universe? Universe maintenance is way out of our hands now; even the archangels can't deal with that one. And if they can't do it, none of the rest of us stand a chance. You know that originally the Sixth Order of angels, the Powers, were supposed to be the keepers of history? Well, every time history changed, they changed with it and *so* couldn't remember anything from before."

Anne looked down at her, "Then why do you remember?"

Henrietta shrugged until her halo lifted clear of her

curls. "I dunno. Being the littlest angel, I seem to get left behind a lot."

Anne's head was back to hurting as she paced from the seeping jars of honey over to the cases of vinegar and pickling spices, and back.

Then she stopped and squinted her eyes at her husband. At a man she had come to love very dearly.

"Which tree are these apples from?"

"Well, my dear Anne, we already have eaten from the Tree of Knowledge. Courtesy of Adam, Eve, and Johnny Appleseed's hard work, those trees now grow all over the Earth."

"These apples are from the Tree of Life," the snake said. "I tried to give an apple from *each* tree to Eve, but the foolish woman couldn't wait to share Knowledge with Adam right away. Then Joshua came in and threw a fit before she could eat of the second tree."

"I was younger then," Joshua struggled in his own defense.

"Threw a fit, banned them from the Garden, *and* left me to crawl in the dirt," Ahv sounded like one very irritated serpent. Well he wasn't the only one.

Anne walked right up to Joshua until they stood nose to nose.

"You banished a *woman* from the Garden of Eden for gaining Knowledge and then wanting to share it?"

Joshua squinted at her in that way he had.

"Oh no," she knew the look.

His eyes shot wide, "I never thought of it that way."

For all of his wonderful powers and kind heart, he

wasn't very well connected to the consequences of his actions.

"Joshua," she managed through gritted teeth.

"I'm sorry, Anne. Seriously, I had no idea. No wonder Eve won't talk to me."

"No wonder."

"What do I do?"

Anne looked at Joshua the One God. A sweet man at a loss for how to undo acts done when he was in one of his rare Old Testament moods.

"You could send her some apples," Henrietta suggested quietly.

Anne was shocked. It was so rare for the angel to say something on point that Anne could only be impressed.

"A great idea, Henrietta. A bit belated, but still an excellent notion."

The little angel glowed until the light off her tiny wings filled the room and competed with the sunshine streaming in through the garden door.

"There are plenty there," Anne turned to Joshua. "We can send half to Eve and still have enough for the Rosh Hashanah dinner."

Joshua nodded happily at her suggestion.

Yet Ahv the Serpent stood on the other side of the door to the Garden of Eden, little more than a sad shadow. All these eons and he'd been left to merely grovel. And garden.

"You never ate of the second tree either?"

Ahv shook his head sadly.

"Don't you think it's about time you had a Life?"

He squinted up at her, "What did you have in mind?"

"I was thinking I'd bake these apples for New Year's dinner. It is the anniversary of the creation of Adam and Eve after all."

"Remember it well," the serpent nodded his head as did Joshua.

"We're supposed to eat apples with honey to bring a sweet New Year. And we have plenty of honey that we need to use up," she pointed toward the seeping jars.

Ahv shook his head and looked down at the apples sadly. "I don't dare cross the threshold. I love my Garden. And if I leave, I've always been afraid that the Cherubim and the flaming sword won't let me return."

"I know! I know!" Henrietta waved a hand over her head and began hopping on one foot atop her apple.

"What?" Anne, Joshua the One God, and Ahv the Serpent asked in unison.

"Easy. The Cherubim got bored eons ago. They're out drinking at this brutish Pictish pub that hasn't been cleaned since Hadrian's Wall was overrun. No one's been guarding the Garden gates since forever." She clapped both hands over her mouth and mumbled out a worried, "Oh gosh! You can't tell that I told you!"

"Why not, Henrietta?" Anne asked as gently as she could.

"If you tell the Seraphim, they'll be very upset with the Cherubim for leaving their post and then the Cherubim will get all angry at me and I'm just a lowly Ninth Choir and I'm—" her voice climbed with each stage of her panic until it threatened to convert the last traces of Anne's headache into a migraine.

"We won't tell," Anne interrupted her and criss-crossed her fingers over her heart. "I promise."

"Oh. Okay." Then Henrietta subsided into a blissful silence and began humming to herself as she polished the apple next to her with the hem of her robe.

"For Rosh Hashanah dinner," Anne decided, "I'm going to use these apples from the Tree of Life to make an Apple Tart of Eden. You're all invited."

She looked directly at Ahv the Serpent.

"All of you. We will all break bread together and share a glass of wine," Anne would have to remember to water Henrietta's; otherwise she got the worst hiccups imaginable. "And we'll toast new beginnings, yes?"

Joshua nodded eagerly and smiled toward Ahv.

The dusty old man directed his smile toward her, the first true smile she'd seen cross his face since she'd met him through the door. He managed to mouth a soft, "Thank you."

Apparently uncomfortable with that, he let the smile slide into a different one that she now knew all too well.

Anne saw the question coming and was already shaking her head no before he asked it.

"Does that mean *now* I get to see your breasts?"

If you enjoyed this, don't miss the novel (excerpt below):
Cookbook from Hell: Reheated

COOKBOOK FROM HELL: REHEATED
(EXCERPT)

*E*ric Erikson answered his cell phone without looking up from his computer screen at work. His desk was a shambles of a half-eaten vending-machine sandwich and too many bags of Fritos.

What blocked number would be calling him at two in the morning on a Friday night? He was just getting down to the second level of tonight's guilty pleasure, indulging in a new Internet role-playing game. He'd gotten in on the beta release of a new project with the weird name of *Chraze* that looked cool, but he wasn't very far into the world yet.

"E-Squared!"

Well, that told him who the caller was. Only his boss, Valerie McKenzie called him that. Everyone else still called him Eric-Squared, for Eric Erikson but she had edited his name down a year ago, before his job interview with Ms. Incredibly Erudite had even ended.

"Hi, Mac." That was the nickname he'd tagged her with during his first week at McKenzie Book Publishers. It had started as "Mac hold the cheese" because one thing about Valerie McKenzie, she wanted it her way. And she got it. She hated New York, so had convinced a major publisher to let her run her own imprint from Seattle. And then, against all projections, she had turned it into a very successful concern.

Now, everyone called her Mac, and "McHell" was a whispered warning that permeated down the halls just moments before she swooped in and touched down like a personalized whirlwind at some poor fool's desk.

"You've got to help me."

Boss in distress. Her voice sounded really wound up, even more than usual. Eyes still glued to the screen, Eric shoved the mouse around to avoid a can of root beer and an unopened bag of peanuts on his desk, barely saving his on-screen avatar from being skewered by a black knight riding a Harley in full armor across a grassy plain in Spain where, according to the stats bar down the side, it hardly ever rained.

"What's up, boss?"

"You know that cookbook?"

No one in the office could avoid "that cookbook." The Mac had torn through the office on a rampage just three days earlier. Mathilda Reeves had finally delivered her latest cookbook manuscript, six weeks late and in miserable shape. The layout team had tried to put it together, but it was a total train wreck. On Wednesday morning, The Mac had grabbed the manuscript, a laptop, and stormed out in order to work from home.

"I know that cookbook." Eric kept his tone carefully neutral. No one had heard from Valerie for three days.

Which had made the office calm and peaceful for a pleasant change of pace. Though he did kind of miss her tornadoing around the thirtieth floor of the Two Union Square building, she certainly kept things interesting.

He whacked the black knight's helmet with a handy caveman cudgel, which he'd bought cheap from an on-screen dealer in Neanderthal artifacts. It made the knight's helmet ring like a church bell. Very satisfying.

"Well, the cookbook now insists that it's looking for God."

That froze his hand on the mouse, at just the wrong moment. The knight gunned the Harley's engine and ran over Eric's figure, flattening him into the sod. Then he circled back and rolled over Eric again crosswise. That sucked. This game handed out some serious retributions when your avatar died.

The Mac took his silence as rapt attention rather than cursing to himself.

"I was working on editing and laying out one of the very last recipes, a typical Mathilda dessert, Flan with Lingonberries. What the Hell is a lingonberry anyway, it's not as if any normal grocery in Hell-and-gone Missouri is going to have them in stock, and suddenly the laptop made a gagging sound, like a loud retching. Next thing I know I'm looking at a recipe titled 'Flogging with Lingonberries' and there's an embedded video of some giant red berry wielding a cat o' nine tails on an apple pie holding up its crust to defend itself. When I tried to hit Undo, the berry turned to me and asked me, *by name,* if I knew where to find God? The thing called me Valerie McKenzie for crying out loud. I'm totally creeped out.

You've gotta help me. I was almost done and I haven't backed up in days."

It was impressive. As far as he could tell, she hadn't taken a single breath in all that.

"Uh, I can try to fix it." He was still trying to piece together the image of a lingonberry knowing its editor's name. And that she'd used words like "totally" as an adverb and "gotta." And contractions. She was rarely desperate enough to use contractions.

"Good, thanks! Can you… Oh God— No! Wait, I didn't mean to say that. Good thing the software can't hear me or it might start asking me more questions."

Eric wondered if she'd been drinking.

"I'm sorry, I didn't notice the time. Could you come by as soon as you can in the morning? I don't care what time. Pretty please, E-Squared?"

Eric had never heard The Mac apologize, let alone beg. He agreed and instantly she was gone.

He looked back at the screen where the black knight had broken into song, singing harmony on a Norse drinking song with the thudding reverberations coming from the Harley's big exhaust pipes, about how he'd been born to be wild. All the while he kept circling around in different directions to run over Eric's figure that foolishly kept trying to get up from his body-shaped hole in the sod. The wheel patterns over the sod were making the shape of an infinity symbol. Eric shut down the game.

One thing for sure, he wasn't going to wait for the morning. He'd never heard The Mac so flustered. Angry? Often. Perhaps too often, though not usually at him. But genuine distress? That was new.

He grabbed his bicycle helmet. He'd ridden in this morning and then stayed at the office to take advantage of the high-speed connection, and the big screen, to beta test the new game. From McKenzie Book Publishers' Westlake Avenue office to Ravenna was only a couple miles and the Seattle streets would be quiet in the middle of the night.

He hit the street and was already moving before he noticed that the pavement was wet. Eric considered going back to get his rain slicks, but it wasn't raining at the moment, so he just downshifted and hurried north along Westlake, past all of the sailboats and houseboats, up to the Fremont Bridge.

He hit the draw bridge and rolled past the sign, "Welcome to Fremont, the center of the Universe. Set your watch back five minutes." The problem he had was that he didn't wear a watch any more. Instead, he used his cell phone that stayed in perfect sync with the cell provider's signal all on its own. Fremont had, through no fault of its own, gone from arcane to archaic and he felt bad on its behalf.

He cut across town on Thirty-Fourth so he could wave at the concrete troll squatting under the Aurora Bridge. The troll had the remains of a VW Beetle clutched in one mighty fist. As usual, he didn't wave back at Eric.

The neighborhoods were all quiet as he sped through. He'd always liked this time of night in Seattle. Most people only saw the bustling city that had doubled in size over the last few decades. But in the middle of the night, there was a silence so deep that he could hear the quiet spatter of his bike tires on the rain-wet streets and the ticking clunks as relay boxes flipped streetlights from red to green just for his passage.

He'd never actually been to The Mac's new apartment. He'd been to the estate she used to have out on Bainbridge Island for last year's Christmas party. A big place filled with canapés and ostentation, that both had and hadn't fit its occupant. Super-editor, The Fearsome Mac, the Woman of Steel, would of course have a sweeping view of Liberty Bay and the Olympic Mountains isolated by large stands of timber along the shore of Port Orchard Bay. And of course she'd be married to some useless guy like Landau McKenzie. He'd been a weird Scottish guy, who looked like a laird and acted like a dweeb. And no sense of humor at all. Not that Mac had one either.

But The Mac had this other side to her, one he spotted only rarely, the human Valerie McKenzie. Sometimes, when exhausted but pleased with herself at shipping off another soon-to-be bestseller, she'd drop by his desk. The woman would collapse in his guest chair and chat for a few minutes. Still perfectly coifed, chestnut-dark hair in a tight French chignon, power suit sharp and expensive, but a smile would emerge and light up her face. Eric had to admit to feeling secretly superior to the rest of the world, as he suspected he was the only one who got to see that life-altering smile.

Everyone else told him he was fantasizing, The Mac never smiled except the way a shark might. So he'd learned to keep his mouth shut, but he'd become more and more intrigued by the Valerie he glimpsed behind The Mac.

Then six months ago she'd divorced Landau Fucking

McKenzie, as she now unfailingly referred to him, and life around the office had really become Hell. Her mood swings had gone from lethal, to chaotic and lethal.

Her current gripe was that changing back to her maiden name wouldn't do any good because she'd "for reasons unknown" thought it cute that she and Landau Fucking McKenzie had the same last name before she was dumb enough to marry him and how in the world could she have ever thought that was charming? Then she'd launch into yet another diatribe on Landau's character.

Eric considered riding north around Green Lake and getting his car, but he was already so close, he just rode to her house on Ravenna. She'd gotten a place just past the shop that had custom-built his road bike, costing him most of a month's pay, over the crest and down toward the park. She lived in a giant Victorian house from Seattle's heyday, now cut up into six or eight apartments.

ERIC ERIKSON HIT the buzzer for Valerie's apartment and got no response.

He considered that it was awfully late, she'd probably gone to bed. Maybe he should go. But she'd sounded so desperate.

He hit the buzzer again, longer and harder.

No voice squawked out of the speaker. But there was click, then a groan, like someone in deep pain. Like someone who'd been stabbed, or worse. When the door release buzzed, he went in fast. He shouldered his bike and bolted up the two flights. He dropped his bike in the hall, leaning it against the sturdy mahogany railing that overlooked the stairwell, and knocked on her door with a fast rat-a-tat.

No response.

He was preparing to test his shoulder against her door locks when he heard the chain drop and the deadbolt being thrown back. The door cracked open and The Mac looked out at him. At least a version of her did. Someone had taken the sharp-edged senior editor and run her through the Photoshop blur tool. Several times.

She blinked at him like a sleepy cat. Rather than pulled back into an immaculate French Roll, her dark dark-red hair, half dry from a shower, snarled about her face and cascaded well past her shoulders. Half of it was caught inside a faded Smith College sweatshirt that might have once been white and gold. It was that oversized thing that women bought for sleeping in. Right now, the too big collar had slipped down to one side and revealed a vast expanse of splendid right shoulder. The sweatpants matched, equally oversized. Her bare feet danced back and forth a bit, the floor was probably cold this time of year, just like at his place.

"Valerie?" This wasn't tougher-than-any-man, The Mac McKenzie.

She blinked those sleep-fogged eyes at him again. He'd never been close enough before to really see them. He knew they were blue, but had never noticed the little flecks of gold. It made him think of calico cats, not super editors. Not of a woman powerful enough to build her own imprint on the West Coast much to the New York publisher's shock.

The Fearsome Mac, tousled. He had to take a steadying breath. It was like having the universe change on you unexpectedly. The fiercest, most driven, and most successful editor in the conglomerate's most profitable imprint never had a single thing out of place. Not a fold of her jacket, not a hair on her head, not a comma in a thousand pages.

Also, he was looking down at her. Normally in serious heels and power suits, she was completely intimidating. Towering over people, even taller ones by sheer intimidation if necessary. Now, barefoot, she stood five-six, five-seven tops. Weird.

"Uh… Hi." She blinked once more and came a little more into focus. "Thanks for coming." She looked at one bare wrist. Then the other. Then she turned slowly in place, stopping when she faced a grandfather clock opposite the door.

"You came fast. I've only slept about twenty minutes. I appreciate it, E-Squared."

Like he'd wait until morning when receiving a panic call from The Mac.

"It's over there." She swung open the door and pointed toward the table.

Most of the apartment was about what he'd expected. Beautiful art on the wall, but rather than investment art, it was mostly soft, Impressionist-style scenes of Italian coasts and French lavender fields that invited you in. Some comfortable chairs, clearly intended for a larger room, but crowded together companionably enough to host a small circle of friends. Light curtains of gold and gray which masked the much heavier curtains of midnight blue needed to cover old apartment windows during the wet Seattle winters. Hardwood that probably dated back a century, complemented by the rosewood-hued pillows on the dusky-aubergine couch.

All very cozy except, taking up a third of the space, an oaken table that would seat eight or ten if it weren't shoved into a corner. Nor was there room to pull it out.

This table, he decided, was all Valerie and very little Mac. It was a disaster worse than his apartment, covered in leftover food wrappers, a delivery pizza box, manuscript pages, and an impressive array of soda cans. He wanted a photograph of this, something to keep in his mind's eye the next time she was busy scaring the shit out of him and everyone else in the office, but he didn't think reaching for his smartphone would be a wise choice.

A trail of clothes led from the chair in front of the computer, past the kitchen and down the hall toward the bathroom. A very intriguing trail. Nice slacks and a simple cashmere sweater that belonged to Mac. A "Come to the Dark Side, We Have Cookies!" t-shirt he wasn't so sure about, since it would imply that The Mac had a sense of humor. And very feminine underwear and bra in pale blue satin that certainly didn't belong in the same time zone as the Woman of Steel.

He did his best to simply take it all in with a single glance then look away. Wouldn't do to be caught staring at his boss' underwear, even if it wasn't on her body.

He edged over to the table and sat, not even removing his jacket. The Mac morphed into a tousled woman who owned sheer, blue satin underwear was giving him problems. And if her underwear was strewn across the oak flooring, what was under the sweats…

He shook his head to clear it.

She'd moved up close behind him, kicking her slacks over to stand on and insulate herself from the cold floor.

"Mathilda Reeves' cookbook is a disaster. I was close, so close. Another ten or twelve hours and I'd have had it ready for the printer, and then it crashed. You have to save me, E-Squared. I hadn't saved in a couple of hours, but I'll deal with that if I have to. I don't have a backup at all, and I'll just completely lose it if I have to redo three days of work. I don't think I can face that. And that lingonberry scared the shit out of me."

He knew that The Mac swore, but he didn't know she had limits. That was news as well.

"Okay, I'll see what I can do." He didn't give voice to his next thought, that he'd be a lot less nervous if she'd move back a few steps and didn't sound so human-woman-in-distress rather than demanding-boss-on-a-tear.

He flipped open the laptop.

An apple-green screen faced him. He hadn't seen one of those in years. It was a normal laptop, but instead of some GUI applications all made for point and click, there was a black screen covered with apple-green question marks in a font like the early DOS days, like in the old mainframes. He wiggled the mouse, but there was no cursor to move around, just the blinking underscore character inviting him to type.

He tapped an enter key.

Nothing.

He typed "exit," but it didn't return to its modern, windowed interface.

He hit control-alt-delete.

The computer flashed a solid screen of bright green at him.

When he'd blinked and could focus on the screen again, he saw a new message there.

Don't do that! I already told her not to do that, but does she listen? Nooo! She just slaps me up the side of my screen, like that's going to jar some electrons loose.

Eric glanced up at Valerie.

She shrugged and whispered, "I was pissed and out of other ideas."

He turned back to the screen.

And now I've got you to deal with? Go away Homo sapien. I've got no more use for you than her...

Unless you happen to know where God is?

"I don't." Eric was so surprised that he typed his response before he'd even thought about it. "In Heaven?"

Nope! Already checked. Not there. Now go away, I'm thinking.

Eric turned to look up at Valerie's gold-flecked eyes. "Uh, this may take a while."

Keep reading at fine retailers everywhere:
Cookbook from Hell: Reheated

ABOUT THE AUTHOR

M.L. Buchman started the first of over 60 novels, 100 short stories, and a fast-growing pile of audiobooks while flying from South Korea to ride his bicycle across the Australian Outback. Part of a solo around the world trip that ultimately launched his writing career in: contemporary romance, military romantic suspense, thrillers, and SF/F.

Recently named in *The 20 Best Romantic Suspense Novels: Modern Masterpieces* by ALA's Booklist, they have also selected his works three times as "Top-10 Novel of the Year." NPR and B&N listed other works as "Best 5 of the Year."

As a 30-year project manager with a geophysics degree who has: designed and built houses, flown and jumped out of planes, and solo-sailed a 50' ketch, he is awed by what's possible. More at: www.mlbuchman.com.

Other works by M. L. Buchman:

<u>White House Protection Force</u>
Off the Leash
On Your Mark
In the Weeds

The Night Stalkers
MAIN FLIGHT
The Night Is Mine
I Own the Dawn
Wait Until Dark
Take Over at Midnight
Light Up the Night
Bring On the Dusk
By Break of Day
WHITE HOUSE HOLIDAY
Daniel's Christmas
Frank's Independence Day
Peter's Christmas
Zachary's Christmas
Roy's Independence Day
Damien's Christmas
AND THE NAVY
Christmas at Steel Beach
Christmas at Peleliu Cove
5E
Target of the Heart
Target Lock on Love
Target of Mine
Target of One's Own

Firehawks
MAIN FLIGHT
Pure Heat
Full Blaze
Hot Point
Flash of Fire
Wild Fire
SMOKEJUMPERS
Wildfire at Dawn
Wildfire at Larch Creek
Wildfire on the Skagit

Delta Force
Target Engaged
Heart Strike
Wild Justice
Midnight Trust

Where Dreams
Where Dreams are Born
Where Dreams Reside
Where Dreams Are of Christmas
Where Dreams Unfold
Where Dreams Are Written

Eagle Cove
Return to Eagle Cove
Recipe for Eagle Cove
Longing for Eagle Cove
Keepsake for Eagle Cove

Henderson's Ranch
Nathan's Big Sky
Big Sky, Loyal Heart
Big Sky Dog Whisperer

Love Abroad
Heart of the Cotswolds: England
Path of Love: Cinque Terre, Italy

Dead Chef Thrillers
Swap Out!
One Chef!
Two Chef!

Deities Anonymous
Cookbook from Hell: Reheated
Saviors 101

SF/F Titles
The Nara Reaction
Monk's Maze
the Me and Elsie Chronicles

Strategies for Success (NF)
Managing Your Inner Artist/Writer
Estate Planning for Authors

Short Story Series by M. L. Buchman:

<u>The Night Stalkers</u>
The Night Stalkers
The Night Stalkers 5E
The Night Stalkers CSAR
The Night Stalkers Wedding Stories

<u>Firehawks</u>
The Firehawks Lookouts
The Firehawks Hotshots
The Firebirds

<u>Delta Force</u>
Delta Force Short Stories

<u>US Coast Guard</u>
US Coast Guard

<u>White House Protection Force</u>
White House Protection Force Short Stories

<u>Where Dreams</u>
Where Dreams Short Stories

<u>Eagle Cove</u>
Eagle Cove Short Story

<u>Henderson's Ranch</u>
Henderson's Ranch Short Stories

<u>Dead Chef Thrillers</u>
Dead Chef Short Stories

<u>Deities Anonymous</u>
Deities Anonymouse Short Stories

<u>SF/F Titles</u>
The Future Night Stalkers
Single Titles

www.ingramcontent.com/pod-product-compliance
Lightning Source LLC
Chambersburg PA
CBHW032053180726
48284CB00004B/1312